Katharine the Almost Great

The Biggest Star by Far

by Lisa Mullarkey
illustrated by Phyllis Harris

visit us at www.abdopublishing.com

To John, Sarah, and Matthew: My biggest stars by far! —LM

To my precious daughter, Emily, who is the "biggest star by far" in my world and soon to be the whole world!! —PH

Published by Magic Wagon, a division of the ABDO Group, 8000 West 78th Street, Edina, Minnesota 55439.

Printed in the United States.

Text by Lisa Mullarkey
Illustrations by Phyllis Harris
Edited by Stephanie Hedlund and Rochelle Baltzer
Interior layout and design by Jaime Martens
Cover design by Jaime Martens

Library of Congress Cataloging-in-Publication Data

Mullarkey, Lisa.
The biggest star by far / by Lisa Mullarkey ; illustrated by Phyllis Harris.
p. cm. -- (Katharine the almost great ; bk. 3)
ISBN 978-1-60270-581-4
[1. Theater--Fiction. 2. Schools--Fiction.] I. Harris, Phyllis, 1962- ill. II. Title.
PZ7.M91148Big 2010
[E]--dc22

2008036099

CONTENTS

WANTED:
ACTORS!
FOR OUR PLAY
"KIDS ROCK
IN SPACE"

CHAPTER 1

Barf-a-Rama Drama

Crockett spotted it first. He rushed over to the poster hanging outside our classroom.

He put his hand on my shoulder. "Too bad you can't be in it—you'd be great."

How true. I *was* a super-duper fab-u-lo-so actor, but nobody besides my stuffed animals and Crockett knew it. Why? Because I have a humongous, ginormous problem: stage fright.

If you have stage fright, you can't read your Earth Day essay out loud even if it won second place in a contest. You can't sing the songs you learned for your grandparents even if they drove hundreds of miles to see you and brought a present.

And if you're supposed to perform in front of strangers, there's only one thing a person with stage fright can do: throw up. So that's what I did. Twice.

My first stage fright freak-out was in kindergarten. I was a jack-in-the-box and was supposed to say, "Welcome to Liberty Corner School." But I refused to pop-a-rooni out of the box. When the curtain finally closed, I ran to the bathroom and barfed.

Then there was the time in first grade when I was a penguin. All I had to do was waddle onto the stage and say, "Baby penguins are called chicks." Easy breezy, right? Wrong! I only waddled three steps before upchucking on Johnny Mazzaratti's feet.

In second grade, I was the Queen of Hearts. I had to search for royal subjects who were performing good deeds in the kingdom. During dress rehearsal, Crockett had to whisper my lines to me.

After that, I just knew that if I got up on stage, it would be kindergarten and first grade all over again. So at breakfast the next day, I announced, "I can't go to school. I'm sick."

Mom felt my forehead. "You don't feel warm."

"I have a disease," I insisted. "Stage fright-itis."

Dad laughed. Mom folded her arms. "Are you afraid to be the Queen of Hearts?"

I shook my head. "I *want* to be in the play. After all, I'm going to be an actor . . . one day."

Dad scratched his head. "Well, here's the thing, Katharine. If you want to be an actor, you have to . . . act."

Mom chuckled. I gave her my grumpy face. It was not a chuckle moment.

Then Dad brought up kindergarten. "You *almost* acted in the kindergarten play."

"And you *almost* acted in your penguin play," added Mom. "But you didn't feel well that day either."

My parents call me Katharine the *Almost* Great. They say I'm a work-in-progress. I bet if I could cure my stage fright, they'd proclaim me a star and call me Katharine the Great.

So I proved to myself that I really was a fab-u-lo-so actor by moaning and groaning so much that they let me stay home. That night, while Crockett became the *King* of Hearts and saved the play, I saved myself from more barf-a-rama drama.

But looking at the *Kids Rock in Space* poster, my stomach did a flip-flop belly drop.

Crockett snapped his fingers. "Earth to Katharine. Come in."

I sighed. "Space can rock without me."

By the time Mrs. Bingsley opened the door, the whole class was buzzin' about the play.

"Who wants to rock in space?" Mrs. Bingsley asked.

Everyone's hand shot into the air. Everyone's but mine.

Mrs. Bingsley looked disappointed. "Katharine?"

I was about to make up some excuse like I was training for the Olympic swim team or I was too busy learning Japanese, when Vanessa, aka Miss Priss-A-Poo, interrupted.

"Katharine's a fraidy cat. Remember how she threw up on Johnny? Remember how she stayed in the box in kindergarten? Remem . . ."

Mrs. Bingsley cut her off. "That was a long time ago, Vanessa. Katharine has a lot to offer our play." Then she added, "All of you do."

"Will everyone have a speaking part?" asked Crockett.

Mrs. Bingsley glanced at me. This is what I thought she'd say:

"Of course. How will anyone ever get over stage fright if they don't get a part?"

But this is what she said:

"Only if they want one. I won't force anyone to do something that makes them uncomfortable."

I felt better until Miss Priss-A-Poo smirked and pretended to throw up on my shoes when Mrs. Bingsley wasn't looking.

"It's a good thing you don't want a part. You might throw up all over the solar system."

Before I knew what I was doing, I blurted out, "I want a part, Mrs. Bingsley."

Crockett looked at me like an alien had invaded my body.

Mrs. Bingsley rubbed her hands together. "Terrific. Now come in and unpack."

Everyone rush-a-rooed inside.

Except me. I skedaddled straight to the nurse's office. My stomach suddenly felt like a rocket was inside ready to blast off.

WANTED:
ACTORS!
FOR OUR PLAY
"KIDS ROCK
IN SPACE"

CHAPTER 2

Penelope Parks to the Rescue

"I'm doomed! Doomed," I moaned. I dumped the bag of popcorn into a bowl. It was Friday night, which meant movie night for Crockett and me.

I shoved the bowl into Crockett's hands and slapped the back of my hand onto my forehead. "I can't eat. I can't sleep. My life is ruined." I pretended to sob. "I can't rock in space."

Crockett laughed. "Looks like you've got the dramatic part down." He threw a piece of popcorn into the air and caught it in his mouth.

"Remember our Christmas play in your room?" He flicked a kernel at me. "And what about the play we put on in the backyard for Fourth of July?" He saluted. "You even sang 'Yankee Doodle, Uncle SamANTHA.'"

I crossed my arms over my chest. "But we didn't have an audience." We had actually put on the shows for my stuffed animals and—in the way, way back—Crockett's lizards, snakes, and tarantula. I don't like creepy crawly fans. Yuck-o!

"I can't have a people audience or I'll freeze like an ice cube," I said.

Crockett walked over to the TV and popped in a DVD. *Penelope Parks and the Mystery of the Lost Dog* scrolled across the screen.

"Not again! We saw this a few weeks ago," I whined. "Why didn't you get the new one?" Not that I minded too much. Penelope Parks solved mysteries with her brother Peter. We'd seen them all at least ten times.

Penelope was pop-pop-popular. Her face was everywhere! She was on posters, notebooks, clothes, backpacks, and even lip gloss. Girls used gobs of it because of her.

Crockett tossed me the DVD case. "Look at the back under Extras. There's an interview with Penelope about acting."

I pressed the menu button. "You're a genius, Crockett!"

Ten seconds later, Penelope and a bald man with a bow tie were sitting on stools in a studio. She wore black boots with glittery laces, a plaid skirt, and a purplicious glittery shirt with a matching headband. Penelope always glitters.

"Look at her, Crockett. I bet she never gets stage fright. She's perfect-o."

"Perfectly fake," Crockett snorted.

Mr. Bow Tie Man started asking questions. "Did you always want to be an actress, Ms. Parks?"

Penelope tossed her hair from side to side and slathered her lips with gloss before answering. "I was born to be an actress. A star. I shine." Then she giggled and covered her mouth.

"Can you remember the first time you acted?" asked Mr. Bow Tie Man. "Did you love it from the moment you stepped onstage?"

She giggled some more. "I'd rather forget my first time on stage," she said as she whipped her hair around.

"I forgot all of my lines and cried. But I was a baby then. Now I *adore* acting. Simply *adore* it."

Penelope batted her eyelashes. "I shine on stage. Simply *shine*." She reached into her pocket and tossed a handful of glitter into the air. "Have some stardust!"

Mr. Bow Tie Man laughed. "It's hard to believe you froze up onstage. You're such a star now. You're loved by millions of children."

Penelope continued giggling and blew a kiss to Mr. Bow Tie Man. "That's sweet of you to say." She crossed her legs.

"I am *adored* by millions and millions of children. There are simply *too* many fans for me to count them all." She looked at the camera, winked, and blew another kiss.

Mr. Bow Tie Man leaned in closer. "Do you have any advice for aspiring actors?"

Penelope puckered her lips and fluffed her hair. "It's all about attitude. If you want to be a star, you must simply *act* like a star."

She stopped talking to apply more gloss. "Even if you're not feeling confident, fake it. After all, you're an actor, aren't you? If you're confident, you'll shine. SHINE!"

Then she reached for Mr. Bow Tie Man's hand. "Here's an autograph." She scribbled her name on his palm and then flashed it to the camera. "Real stars don't wait until someone *asks* for an autograph. We give it automatically to show our appreciation."

Mr. Bow Tie Man thanked her. "Well, you certainly do shine, Ms. Parks. How do you do it?"

She flashed a super-duper mega smile. "Start by smiling, dah-ling. Smile, smile, smile." Then she pointed to her shirt. "You like? To shine, you need to be glittery and glowy. Sparkly. Shimmery. Dazzly."

Then Penelope stared directly into the camera. "So check out my new clothing line for ages eight and up, available in stores everywhere."

With that, the interview was over.

But my career as *Katharine the Biggest Star by Far* was just about to begin.

CHAPTER 3

A Star Is Born

On Saturday morning, I tiptoed into Jack's room and sang "Twinkle Twinkle Little Star" to him. Then I spoke in my very best Penelope voice.

"Good morning, dah-ling. You're simply an adorable baby. *Adorable* I tell you."

I tossed my hair from side to side just like Penelope. "Would you like me to read to you?" I flipped through his bookcase and pulled out a book with a sparkly cover. "Look, Jack. This cover is sparkly. It's shiny and glowy and glimmery. Just like . . . me!"

When I went to the kitchen for breakfast, my parents started humming "Twinkle Twinkle."

"You're simply an adorable singer, dah-ling," said Mom. "You shine."

Dad pointed to the baby monitor. "And glow and glimmer and sparkle."

My cheeks burned. But then I remembered what Penelope had said. If you don't *feel* confident, *fake* it. So I did.

I started singing every song I could think of from "Row, Row, Row Your Boat" to "Here We Go 'Round the Mulberry Bush."

The more Jack squealed and kicked his feet and cooed, the louder I got. Within five minutes, Aunt Chrissy and Crockett had trudged upstairs to see what all the fuss-a-roo was about.

That afternoon, I transformed my clothes into Penelope look-alikes thanks to Aunt Chrissy's glitter.

"How much of this stuff do you need?" asked Crockett as he held a basket packed with itty-bitty bottles.

"All of it," I said as I swiped the container from him. "I need to shine. *Shine* I say."

I tossed him one of my shirts. "Want to help?" I batted my eyelashes the way Penelope batted hers. "Pretty, pretty please?"

"No can do. I'm playing basketball with Johnny."

I dropped a bottle of glitter onto the bed. "Really? You'd actually pick Johnny over me?" I grabbed a tissue and dabbed my eyes. "I thought you were more than just my cousin. I thought you were a . . . a . . . a friend."

Crockett stammered. "Don't be mad, Katharine. I mean, I just don't want to sit here and make girly clothes."

"Gotcha!" I yelled. "Ha!" My acting ability amazed even me!

Crockett rolled his eyes and chucked the shirt at me.

For dinner, Dad took us all to Wing Li's Chinese Restaurant. After dessert, I clanked my fork against my glass. "I have an announcement." I whipped out my Luscious Lemon Lip Gloss and slowly slathered it on.

Dad glanced at his watch.

"I insist," I said dramatically, "on leaving the tip for the waitress."

My parents laughed. Mom asked, "Did you rob your bank?"

I shook my head. "I'm not leaving money. I'm leaving something much more valuable."

I reached inside my pocket, pulled out a folded piece of paper, and dropped it onto the table. "It's my autograph. It'll be worth millions one day."

Dad raised his eyebrow. This is what I thought he'd say:

"We'll never have to tip anyone ever again."

But this is what he really said:

"Don't be silly." And then he tossed a five dollar bill on top.

When Aunt Chrissy took Crockett and me to the store on Sunday, I grabbed my emergency stash of moola. I planned on buying oodles of Penelope Parks lip gloss. We ran into Miss Priss-A-Poo checking out the DVDs.

"Hi, Vanessa," said Aunt Chrissy. "Buying a movie?"

Vanessa waved and nodded. "I'm looking for a Penelope Parks movie. My mom said that I deserve a special treat since I won the recipe contest at school."

She picked up *Penelope Parks and the Mystery of the Stolen Treasure*. Then her eyes lit up as she grabbed *Penelope Parks and the Mystery of the Lost Dog*. "I've been dying to see this one."

It was the one with Penelope's acting tips! I grabbed it out of her hand. "Trust me, Vanessa. You DO NOT want to see this one."

Miss Priss-A-Poo twirled her hair around her finger and glanced at the rack. She stomped her foot. "Oh, I get it. You want the last one for yourself."

Aunt Chrissy was busy plunking things into her basket. As she zip-a-zoomed down the aisle, I leaned in close to Vanessa. "I already have this one, don't I, Crockett?"

"Yep. We've watched it about five times."

Miss Priss-A-Poo shot her nose into the air. "Then it must be good."

"Well, the dog . . . it's really sad . . . something happens . . ." Then I made my eyes get all watery. "No, I can't . . ." I looked at Crockett. "You tell her."

Crockett shoved his hands into his pockets. "I'm not going to tell her. You tell her. It's too sad."

Vanessa shrieked. "Does the dog die? I can't watch sad movies." She dropped the DVD back on the rack, snatched a different Penelope Parks movie, and stormed off.

Aunt Chrissy wandered back and gave us her grumpy, grumpy eyes. "Why did you tell her that something sad happens to the dog?"

Did her ears have special powers? Luckily, I had a cool calendar with 365 useless facts that came in handy during times like this. "Did you know that a Labrador retriever is the most popular dog in the United States?"

She wasn't impressed. I gave her my very most innocent look. "Did I say anything sad happened to the dog?"

Aunt Chrissy bit her lip. "No, I suppose you didn't. But you acted upset. Your eyes watered."

Crockett tossed a pack of gum into the cart and patted me on the back. "She's an actor."

I bowed and went to pay for my lip gloss. At the checkout counter, I spied a picture of Penelope on a magazine cover and thought about her interview. "*Even if you're not feeling confident, fake it. If you're confident, you'll shine. SHINE!*"

I winked and blew magazine Penelope a kiss. I tossed my hair from side to side.

Then I yawned. Who knew shining could be so exhausting?

CHAPTER 4

Glitter Girl

Mom plunked a plate of pancakes on the table. "Eat up. You want to start the school week off right."

I sniff-a-rooed the air. "I adore pancakes, mother. They smell delicious." I batted my eyelashes and pointed to my shirt. "You like?" I had used purplicious glitter to decorate it Penelope-style.

"I'm shining, mother, aren't I? I adore shining and glittering and being glowy."

Mom nodded, "Yes, *daughter*, I like." She laughed.

And when I saw her sneaking a peek at my super-duper glittery sneakers, I lifted my foot up so she could get a closer look.

This is what I thought she'd say:

"They're beautiful! Make me a pair!"

But this is what she really said:

"Katharine Marie Carmichael. What were you thinking? You've ruined your good sneakers."

My stomach did a flip-flop belly drop. "Did you know that Vermont has a stinky sneaker contest every year?"

She pointed to my feet. "Are they wet?"

I jumped up. "Nope." I dragged my finger across the front. "Just glittery." I spun around. "Penelope Parks is perfect, Mom. She says you have to shine, shine, shine." I swirled and twirled in circles. "So, I sparkle, sparkle, sparkle."

Mom sighed. "Be yourself, Katharine. Penelope is a good actor, but she isn't someone I'd want as a daughter."

She grabbed a napkin and blotted my lips. "And she wears entirely too much lip gloss." She inspected my sneakers. "Promise me that you'll ask permission before creating any more Penelope-type crafts."

"Okey dokey," I said as I twirled one last time. Jack clapped his hands. I bowed.

Mom frowned and brushed a piece of glitter off her shoulder. "Not only are *you* shining, Katharine. So is the floor, the table, your pancakes, and Jack's high chair! Get the dustpan and sweep up this mess."

I gave her my very best horrified look. "Actors act, mother. We don't sweep."

"Katharine, lose the attitude. Don't be disrespectful."

I grabbed the dustpan and brush. "No problem, dah-ling." I blew her a kiss.

"Katharine!" Mom's voice definitely sounded thundery now.

Just then, Crockett came bouncing up the steps and tossed his backpack onto the table. "Hey, Jack." He flicked a fleck of purple glitter out of Jack's hair and turned to me. "Hi, Penelope."

"I'm not Penelope," I reminded him. "I'm just trying to *act* like her."

He looked me up and down and gave me a goof-a-roo grin. "Is today Dare to Be Different Day again?"

I stuck my tongue out. "Ha, ha."

After I gobbled down the pancakes and plucked glitter out of my eyebrows, Crockett and I walked to school. When we got there, kids were already huddled around Mrs. Bingsley asking questions about the play.

"We'll pick names out of a hat during morning meeting," said Mrs. Bingsley. Then she clapped her hands. "Time to unpack."

At morning meeting, Miss Priss-A-Poo complained that my shirt was snowing glitter and piling up all over her sweater. So I inched back a row. But then Rebecca moaned that my glitter was ruining her boots.

I glanced at her boots. They were real Penelope Parks boots with glittery laces. Only her glitter didn't peel off.

So I scooted back a few more inches.

"Let's see if I have this correct," said Mrs. Bingsley. She held up a hat. "Everyone wants a part?"

All the kids stared at me. I got that rocket-blasting-off feeling again.

Fake it, I thought. "I sure do. I *adore* school plays. Simply *adore* them."

Crockett laughed.

"Our play is a musical," Mrs. Bingsley continued. "So, some of you may have a small solo and others will sing in a group."

Sing? In front of people? My stage fright-itis poked me in the stomach.

Miss Priss-A-Poo crawled back to me. "You know, Katharine, I heard Mrs. Bingsley changed the title of the play."

"Really?" I asked. "It's not *Kids Rock in Space*?"

"Nope," said Miss Priss-A-Poo. "It's now called *Glitter Girl Hurls through Space*." Johnny laughed. I ignored her and coated my lips with gobs of Berrylicious Bubblegum gloss.

It only took five minutes for everyone's parts to be handed out. Vanessa was Mars.

She clapped and jumped up and down. “My brother said there are aliens on Mars!”

“Then you’ll fit right in,” said Johnny.

For that funny joke, I planned on giving Johnny two autographs.

“For the part of the sun,” said Mrs. Bingsley as she reached into the hat, “Katharine.”

Now it was my turn to jump up and down. *The sun.* The most perfect-o, fab-u-lo-so part.

It was a *star,* after all.

The brightest star by far!

Now all I had to do was keep my lunch out of orbit.

CHAPTER 5

Stardust and Sassitude

Practices were easy breezy! There wasn't a rocket rumble in my stomach all week. At least, not until Mrs. Bingsley announced that our next practice would be on the gym's stage.

My heart pounded. "Mrs. Bingsley, our room is very comfy cozy, isn't it?"

She glanced around the room. "I've worked hard to make it this way. Thanks for noticing!"

"I've been thinking . . . why go to the ginormous gym when we have a perfectly good room here?"

"Our room isn't large enough," said Mrs. Bingsley. "Your parents, friends . . . the whole Liberty Corner School community will be attending."

The whole Liberty Corner School community? I squeezed my eyes shut and crossed my fingers hoping it wouldn't be barf-a-rama drama all over again.

"Katharine, are you feeling okay?" asked Mrs. Bingsley. "You look pale."

"Are you getting ready to barf?" whispered Miss Priss-A-Poo in a voice too low for Mrs. Bingsley to hear.

I wanted to say this:

"I'm having mega major freak-a-rama drama. I can't go onstage. I'll be doomed. Doomed!"

But then I thought of Penelope Parks and said this instead:

"I'm fine, Mrs. Bingsley. I just *adore Kids Rock in Space* and simply *can't* wait until the big day."

I was glad when Mrs. Bingsley gave us free reading time a few minutes later. I rushed over to the purplicious beanbag chair so I could figure out exactly how many people were in the whole Liberty Corner School community.

Miss Priss-A-Poo skipped over. "If you're nervous, I know a trick that will help you calm down."

"Go away," I barked. I didn't believe her.

"No, really," Miss Priss-A-Poo insisted. "I saw it on a Penelope Parks video."

I bit my lip. "What is it?" I was ready for another disgust-o joke.

"It's easy." She motioned for me to scoot over. "Breathe deep, count to ten, and then exhale."

So I did.

And then I did it again. And again. And again.

For the next five minutes, Vanessa and I sat squished side-by-side on the purplicious beanbag and practiced sucking in air.

Although I felt an itty-bitty dizzy, it worked. I felt better.

Before Vanessa got up, I reached for a marker from the art center. I grabbed her script and scribbled:

To Vanessa,

Thanks for the tip. You'll make a great Mars.

From Katharine,
The Biggest Star By Far

She read it and frowned. "*I'm* the biggest star by far." She skipped back to her desk.

After mega math problems, it was lunchtime. As soon as I got to the cafeteria, I headed straight to the buyers' line. Now that Mom worked here, she let me buy lunch two days a week.

Today's special was Breakfast for Lunch, which was Vanessa's winning entry in the recipe contest.

I grabbed a tray. "Special number one, please."

The cafeteria lady, Mrs. Clarkson, looked up. "Hi, Katharine. Your mom told me you're playing the sun in a play."

"Yep," I said. "And you know what the sun does, don't you?" Kids started nudging me forward.

She shrugged. "What?"

"Shines," I said as I flashed my best Penelope Parks smile and tossed my hair from side to side. "And you know what that means, don't you?"

She shrugged again. "What?"

"It means I'm a star. Get it? A *star*? The sun is a star. I'm going to be the biggest star by far!" I reached into my pocket, pulled out some glitter and threw it into the air. "Here's some stardust for you."

Crockett was getting impatient. "Come on, Katharine. We don't have all day."

I slammed my tray down. "An actress cannot be rushed."

I whipped out my lip gloss and was about to slather it on when I felt a tap-tap-tap on my shoulder. When I turned around, I came face-to-face with Principal Ammer, aka *Ammer the Hammer*.

Someone yelled, "You got nailed!"

Then my mom came out of her office and saw Mrs. Ammer's grumpy, grumpy eyes and red, red cheeks.

"What's going on?" she asked. Then she noticed the sparkly glitter on the oranges, apples, and bananas. She gasped. "Katharine, you didn't!"

Mrs. Ammer pursed her lips. "She did."

"I'm just showing a little attitude," I said. "Like Penelope."

Mrs. Ammer frowned. "No, Katharine. You've got much more than an attitude. You have a bad case of sassitude." She picked up my tray. "Let's have lunch together."

She looked like she needed a happy face tattoo.

I gulped. "Did you know that the first cafeteria was built in Kansas City, Missouri, in 1891?"

She wasn't listening. "You do know where we're going, don't you?" she asked as she walked toward the doors.

"Um . . . to a galaxy far, far away?"

She didn't smile.

I suddenly felt like a falling star.

CHAPTER 6

Will the Real Katharine Please Stand Up?

Mrs. Ammer set my tray on the table in her office. "Eat," she ordered.

I glanced at the refrigerator in the corner of the room. "Do you have any milk?" I asked, as I fluff-a-puffed my hair. "I simply adore chocolate milk. Don't you?"

Mrs. Ammer bit her lip and looked me up and down. "By chance, are you trying to imitate Penelope Parks? My granddaughter loves Penelope. Me? I'm not too sure."

I squealed. "Oooh, I *adore* Penelope." I pointed to my glittery shirt and put my foot on the table to show off my sparkly sneakers. "She's helped me shine, shine, shine!"

Mrs. Bingsley looked at my foot like it was covered with creepy crawlers. I quickly took it off the table. "Sorry."

"And why are you acting more like Penelope these days instead of being yourself?"

So I told her all about my stage fright-itis and how I just knew I'd get sick again unless I could fake my confidence and shine.

Then I told her how Vanessa thought I would hurl in space. "I don't want to mess up again, like I did in kindergarten and first grade. If Penelope can do it, I can too."

"Penelope is a lot older than you, Katharine. When she was your age, her stage fright was so bad, she locked herself in a bathroom on a movie set. It took her a long time to get over it."

It was funny picturing Penelope stuck in the bathroom like I was stuck in the box.

"She said she only forgot her lines once. Just once."

Mrs. Ammer nodded. "That's probably true, but she was so scared of performing onstage, that she froze and couldn't move." She handed me a napkin.

"Just like you did in the box in kindergarten." She grabbed a brown bag out of the fridge. "Did you know that she was supposed to star as Annie on Broadway but backed out on opening night?"

My mouth dropped open. "Opening night? Just like me in first grade!" I scratched my head. "But why didn't she just fake it?"

"She probably discovered that secret after her Broadway flop," said Mrs. Bingsley. "But look at her now."

Mrs. Ammer sure did know a lot about Penelope Parks. I just had to ask, "How do you know so much about Penelope Parks? Have you been watching the Extras on her DVDs?"

"Nope," she snickered. "Penelope has way too much sassitude for my liking. It's quite obvious that you've been watching the Extras. You've been picking up a little sassitude yourself."

Then she pursed her lips. "I don't like sassitude, Katharine. I do not adore it at all, dah-ling."

I smiled. Mrs. Ammer didn't.

She continued, "What I do like, is the Katharine I've known and admired over the last four years. Besides, Penelope's friends think she's a brat."

Mrs. Ammer patted my shoulder. "And no one wants their friends to think they're bratty."

She was bursting my Penelope Parks bubble.

"So, how *do* you know so much about Penelope?" I asked.

"I read a lot, Katharine. My granddaughter gets all the teen magazines. And my brother is a cameraman who has worked with Penelope about a dozen times."

I shoved my napkin in front of her. "Maybe you can get me her autograph?"

❀ ❀ ❀

When I went outside for recess, everyone zip-a-zoomed over to see me.

"Are you okay? Your mom sure did look mad," said Crockett.

"Thunder and lightning mad?" I asked.

"Worse," said Johnny. "She was so upset, she kept apologizing and went to talk to Mrs. Bingsley."

"Well," said Vanessa. "Did Ammer the Hammer nail you?"

I wanted everyone to think I wasn't really in trouble. I was going to say this:

"Mrs. Ammer said she simply adored me and wanted to have lunch with the biggest and brightest star by far."

But then I remembered what Mrs. Ammer said about Penelope's friends thinking she was bratty. This is what I really said:

"She told me that she likes Katharine Carmichael a lot more than she likes Penelope Parks." And then I looked down. "Sorry."

"For what?" asked Johnny.

"For acting . . .," I searched for the right word.

"Bratty?" said Crockett. "Snotty? Dopey?" He tossed me the ball. "It's okay. We'll forgive you, as long as you go back to being you."

For the next 20 minutes, I worked extra hard to prove I wasn't a bratty actor anymore. I passed the basketball to Tamara instead of taking the shot myself. When I double dribbled, I called it on myself. I let Crockett get all the rebounds. By the end of recess, I was pretty sure I was brat-free.

When I got home, Mom was waiting for me on the porch. "Hi, Mom."

She didn't say anything.

I could tell she was mucho mega mad. "Did you know that basketball became an official Olympic event at the

Summer Games in Berlin, Germany, in 1936?"

She opened the door. "Start your homework. We'll talk about manners, sassitude, and Penelope Parks after dinner."

I sat at the kitchen table and pulled my folder out of my backpack. I separated the papers into two piles. In one pile I put the notes for my parents. The other pile was homework sheets.

On the tip-top of the parents pile, there was a flyer about picture day tomorrow.

Mom saw it and snapped, "Don't even think about wearing glitter tomorrow."

"No more glitter," I said. "Promise." Then I did my homework and thought about what Mrs. Ammer had said during my lunch visit.

By the time I finished my homework, I had thought of a way to make tomorrow extra, extra special for all the kids in the play.

We'd *all* shine and we wouldn't need a speck of glitter to sparkle!

CHAPTER 7

Picture Perfect

That night my parents had ice cream sundaes for dessert. They are my absolute favoritest treat. But instead of dessert, I got a talking-to.

"Katharine, your mom said you were rude today," said Dad. He took a deep breath. "I'm sure there are other kids who are nervous about the play. And think about how hard Mrs. Bingsley's been working. When did *Kids Rock in Space* become all about you, you, you?"

I hadn't thought about that. I got all squirmy. Everyone had been working hard. I turned toward Mom. "I'm sorry. I was a brat-a-rooni. A big brat-a-rooni who's afraid to hurl in space."

"If you're that nervous, you don't have to be in it," Mom said. "Mrs. Bingsley would understand."

"Not be in the play? But I can't let everyone down." I looked at Dad. "Dad's right. It's not just about me, me, me anymore."

I thought about telling them my idea but decided to keep it a secret. They might not think it's quite as super-duper as I do. "I know I can do it, Penelope says . . ."

Mom put her fingers on my lips. "No more Penelope. We have faith in you and you should too." She picked Jack up off the floor. "About your punishment for throwing glitter and for your sassitude . . ."

I crossed my fingers. This is what I wanted her to say:

"Going up onstage and dealing with stage fright is punishment enough."

But this is what she really said:

"I wouldn't let Mr. Bollwage clean up your glittery mess in the cafeteria. Tomorrow morning, you'll sweep it all up and wash the glitter out of the fruit bowls. That should not be the custodian's job. Got it?"

I nodded.

"And, you're never to touch glitter again," Dad said. Then he hugged me. "Unless Penelope asks you to help her design her clothing line. Got it?"

"Okey dokey," I said.

Mom handed Jack to Dad. "Now, go lay out your good clothes for picture day."

I skedaddled up the stairs. My parents were right. It wasn't just about me, me, me. I decided I was going to prove it. And my idea was the perfect way to show everyone.

Ten minutes after I started my top secret project, Crockett knocked on my door. "What'cha doing?"

I told him all about my plan. "I want to thank Mrs. Bingsley for making *Kids Rock in Space* for us. So, I want to take a picture of our class tomorrow at picture day and give it to her. It will be a perfect-o picture. Want to help?"

Crockett waved his hands. "No way, Katharine. I'm not getting involved in any of your glittery ideas."

I held up a marker. "No glitter. Just markers. I'm making a poster for each part of the play. We can hold up our poster so Mrs. Bingsley will always remember who had what part."

Crockett came over and glanced at the two finished posters.

"These look great. But maybe you should use black markers to outline everything so it shows up better."

Crockett always had fab-u-lo-so ideas. I sure was relieved that he decided to help after all.

When we finished, we stood back to admire our masterpieces. "Perfect-o," I said. "Mrs. Bingsley will be surprised."

"If it works," said Crockett.

"How can it not?" I asked.

❀ ❀ ❀

Right away the next morning, Crockett talked to our art teacher, Mrs. Dee. She agreed to make a banner for our picture.

"It'll look great in the background!" said Mrs. Dee. "I'll work on it right away so it's dry for your class's picture time this afternoon."

During lunchtime, I brought the posters outside and filled everyone in on the plan.

"Mrs. Bingsley is going to love it," said Tamara.

"The posters look pretty," said Vanessa.

"You spelled my name wrong," said Johnny. I grabbed the poster. Johnny laughed. "Just kidding."

When Mrs. Bingsley marched us down to the gym for our pictures at two fifteen, we were revved up and ready.

Mrs. Dee met us at the door. "Mrs. Bingsley, you must have a zillion things to do before the play tomorrow. I'll bring your class back when Mr. Ling is finished."

"I do have a lot left to do. Thank you!" said Mrs. Bingsley. Then, she zip-a-zoomed away from the gym.

Mr. Ling was Rebecca's father. After the coast was clear, Rebecca explained our plan to her dad. A minute later, he gave us the thumbs-up sign.

So Mrs. Dee hung the banner. Crockett and I passed out the posters one by one as the kids climbed onto the risers. Everyone shuffled into their spot and got ready.

"Looking spiffy," said Mr. Ling. "On the count of three say *Kids Rock in Space*. One, two, three!"

"KIDS ROCK IN SPACE!" we shouted.

"Let me take one more just to be sure," said Mr. Ling. He fiddled with the camera. *"Say, Man on the Moon."*

"MAN ON THE MOON!"

As we lined up to leave, Rebecca and Mr. Ling came over to me. "I'll have a copy of the picture tonight," said Mr. Ling. "Will you have time to finish the project?"

Crockett shook his head. "We have swimming lessons tonight."

Darn. We had missed last week's lessons. There was no way my mom would ever let me miss two weeks in a row.

Vanessa overheard. "I don't have anything tonight. I can get the picture and finish the project. I know just what to do."

I bit my lip. The plan was *my* idea and I wanted to be the one to make it happen. This is what I wanted to say:

"No way!"

But then I remembered this wasn't all about me, me, me. This is what I really said:

"Thank you, Vanessa. That would be great."

It better be.

Mercury
COMET
MOON
SUN
SATURN
MARS

CHAPTER 8

The Grand Finale

I shouldn't have. But I did. I took a quick peek-a-roo through the curtains.

The gym was stuffed like a stocking at Christmas. I spotted my parents and Aunt Chrissy in the first row talking. They were probably wondering if I'd shine . . . or barf.

I jumped off the risers and tapped Mrs. Bingsley's shoulder. "I'm doomed. Doomed! My stage fright's back."

Mrs. Bingsley pulled me close. "You'll be fine. Just have fun."

Easy breezy for her to say.

Fun was watching Penelope Parks movies with Crockett. Fun was baking cookies with Mom and adding extra chip-a-roos to the batter. Fun was making crafty fashions with glitter. Performing and singing in front of 500 people? Not fun.

The rest of the solar system looked ready to rock. Johnny was adjusting his rings. Tamara was singing her solo, "Mission Control," to Rebecca. Crockett was reciting his lines.

I *tried* practicing my lines, but how can you practice when you can't even remember them? Was the sun 93 million miles away from Earth or 39 million miles away? Was the sun four and a half *billion* years old or four and a half *trillion* years old? A drop of sweat trickled down my face. How did Penelope Parks make it look so easy?

Mrs. Bingsley flashed the lights, which signaled that the show was starting.

As the curtain opened, cameras flashed. Then the music started and my class belted out "Kids Rock in Space."

Except for me.

I didn't sing. I didn't do the rocka-rocka arm motions. My stomach felt rumbly. It was kindergarten and first grade all over again.

Until Miss Priss-A-Poo leaned forward. "Breathe." Then she added, "Close your eyes."

Huh?

She poked me in the shoulder. "Close your eyes and sing."

So I shut my eyes and joined in on the third verse. Rocka-rocka went my arms to the right. Rocka-rocka went my arms to the left. When the song ended, an explosion of applause erupted.

I opened one eye. Then the other. A zillion people stared back as Rebecca walked to the microphone and welcomed everyone to show. I clamped my eyes shut again. If I was going to make this work, it would have to be in the dark.

But how could I find my microphone, say my lines, and find Matthew in his moon costume with my eyes closed?

The music for our next song blasted through the speakers. I belted out "Asteroids and Meteors and Comets! Oh My!" with no problem and then launched into "The Milky Way Rock."

Then came my cue. My knees shook. I stepped off the risers, squeezing my eyes even tighter. I took a baby step forward. Then another and another.

I slowly reached out, hoping I'd feel the microphone and wouldn't send it crashing to the floor. It was there!

I leaned forward and said my first line, "Did you know that the sun is really just a star?" And then all my lines just pop, pop, popped out of my mouth! No flubbing!

Then I had to stand there while Matthew spoke into the microphone on the opposite side of the stage. He forgot one line, but no one seemed to notice.

After he finished, we had to spin toward each other and meet in the middle of the stage to make a partial and total eclipse.

With my eyes still closed, I stepped to the right and held out my hands in case I was about to bump into something . . . or someone.

I twirled and twirled and almost twirled right past Matthew, but he grabbed me and shoved me behind him for the total eclipse. Everyone clapped. Then, I moved a few inches to the left and made the partial eclipse.

Everyone clapped again.

Now all I had to do was get back to my seat. But where was I? Did I walk straight back? Diagonal? I froze. The audience laughed.

I finally opened my eyes and looked to the left. No Matthew. I looked to the right. No Matthew. I was all alone on stage. I did a quicky quick wave and zip-a-zoomed back to my spot.

My part was over! I did it! For the rest of the play, I kept my eyes open.

When the play ended, Mrs. Bingsley thanked everyone for their hard work. This was the cue for Crockett and Vanessa to step forward. When they did, Mrs. Bingsley looked confused.

Crockett read from an index card. "Dear Mrs. Bingsley, we wanted to thank you for writing this awesome play, making our costumes, and giving us a chance to rock out in space."

Then Vanessa spoke. "Our class would like to give this to you because we think *you* rock."

As she handed Mrs. Bingsley the picture frame, Mr. Ling and Mrs. Dee rolled out a ginormous poster of our class picture. It was so big that the whole audience could see it.

In the picture, each of us held our posters that represented our parts. We each signed our name under our picture. The banner that Mrs. Dee made was behind us. It said: *Mrs. Bingsley Is Out of this World!*

Mrs. Bingsley touched her heart. "Thank you all so much. I'm honored to be your teacher. Everyone did such a wonderful job tonight that I'm already writing our next play for the spring. There's a lot more singing. Even dancing!"

My stomach did a flip-flop belly drop.

Then she turned toward us. "But remember, I'd never make students do anything that made them uncomfortable."

I had no idea if my stomach could handle another play. But I did know one thing for sure.

Mrs. Bingsley was the biggest star by far!

Beat Your Stage Fright-itis!

Katharine isn't the first person to get stage fright! You may have experienced a flip-flop belly drop before a dance recital, school concert, or play. Next time you get nervous about performing, follow these tips to beat stage fright-itis:

1. Practice your piece in front of a group of people before the big event. This practice will help you be prepared and be confident when the big day comes!
2. Imagine the audience in funny costumes. This will make the audience less scary.
3. Take a deep breath. Hold it for ten seconds. Then slowly breathe out. This breathing pattern slows your heartbeat and helps you relax.
4. Remember to have fun! You don't have to be a fab-u-lo-so actor or dancer. Just be you and you'll be a star!